The Gunslinger of Boerne

In the heart of Texas,
a gunslinger laid down his past and built a future

Forward

This book, "The Gunslinger of Boerne," is a work of fiction. While the town of Boerne, Texas, is a real place with a rich history, the characters, events, and situations depicted within these pages are products of the author's imagination. Any resemblance to actual persons, living or dead, or real-life occurrences is purely coincidental. This is a story spun from the spirit of the Old West, intended solely for entertainment.

By Richard Dell Schwarz

Chapter One: The Long Ride South

The sun hung low and angry over the Texas horizon, burning the sky in shades of crimson and gold. Dust clung to every crease in James Butler Hickok's coat, his long hair stiff from weeks of wind and sweat. He hadn't spoken to a soul in two days, not since he'd left the bitter remains of a poker game gone wrong in Abilene. Another fight, another corpse, another town behind him. The West was changing—and so was he.

He rode a tall, chestnut gelding with a bad temper and good instincts, named him Jonah for the trouble he seemed to attract. Together, they followed no trail, just the steady pull of south and silence. Hickok wasn't running, not exactly. But he wasn't chasing anything either. Not fortune. Not glory. He'd had those. They never stayed.

By mid-afternoon, the hills began to change—rolling limestone ridges broke up the flat Texas sprawl, dotted with live oaks and thick cedar. It was the kind of land that made a man wonder if peace could grow here. But Hickok knew better than to believe in peace. He'd seen too much war, too many outlaws, too much blood soaked into too many front porches.

He passed through small settlements on the way south—mostly dusty crossroads towns with one-room churches, wandering chickens, and more fear than hope in the eyes of the people. Occasionally, someone recognized him. They never said anything. Not out loud. But there was always a look—part fear, part curiosity, and part a desperate plea that he move on.

Hickok obliged. He always did. He was tired of being someone to talk about. Even more tired of being someone to fear.

He spent one night in a barn outside of Johnson City, huddled in straw while a thunderstorm cracked the heavens wide open. The rain soaked through the boards, pooling at his feet. He didn't sleep. Just sat there with his back against the wood, revolver on his lap, eyes flicking to every sound. He used to sleep like a stone. Now every noise made him tense.

The next day, he turned west, following a trader's advice about a quiet little place in the hills where German immigrants had built a town called Boerne. "Good beer, strong folk, and no interest in shootouts," the man had said, hitching his wagon. Hickok nodded. Maybe that's what he needed—a town with no interest in men like him.

At the crest of a gentle slope, he reined Jonah in. Below, tucked between the folds of the hills, was a little town—a steeple, a windmill, and a cluster of stone buildings that looked European in style, with sharp roofs and shuttered windows. A sign near the road read "Boerne," painted in careful letters and framed with wildflowers. It looked almost like something from a storybook. Unreal. Untouched.

Hickok tilted his hat back. "Well, Jonah," he muttered, "Let's see if they got decent whiskey... and no damn trouble."

He guided Jonah down the path, passing a group of children who stopped their game to stare. One of the boys pointed at his pistols. Another whispered something and was quickly hushed by a girl who looked like she'd been told stories about gunslingers and wasn't sure whether to be impressed or afraid. Hickok gave them a slight nod and kept moving.

As he entered the town proper, he noticed how different Boerne felt. The streets were quiet but not tense. A woman swept her stoop while humming a lullaby. A man hammered a horseshoe into shape, the clang echoing in the air. The buildings were clean, the stonework solid and enduring. Boerne was no boomtown. It was made to last.

Outside the general store, a girl of about seventeen swept the stone steps and watched him approach. She paused, broom in hand, eyes narrowed with a kind of wary curiosity. She had the look of someone raised with rules, someone who had seen enough newcomers to know the difference between a trader and a troublemaker.

"Something wrong with your eyes?" she asked, her voice crisp, the German accent like a trace of music behind her words.

Hickok tipped his hat. "Just ain't used to seeing anyone so... upright."

She rolled her eyes and walked past him, but he caught the faintest trace of a smirk on her lips. There was fire there—something alive.

He filed her away in his mind as he tethered Jonah outside the saloon.

Inside, the air was thick with cigar smoke, the kind that clung to your clothes for days. A violin player sat hunched in the corner, coaxing out a sad tune while a few old-timers nursed their beers. Hickok walked up to the bar and ordered a whiskey. No small talk. Just a quiet drink.

The barkeep was a squat man with thick arms and a thicker accent. He poured without asking questions but studied Hickok all the same.

"You're not the first gunman we've seen come through," he said after a long pause. "But you'd be wise to mind your temper here. Folks in Boerne work hard to keep things quiet."

Hickok smiled without humor. "Quiet's what I'm lookin' for."

He drank slowly, watching the room without seeming to. No one challenged him. No one offered him a game of cards. That was good. The last time he'd sat for cards, it had ended with blood on the floor and a sheriff calling him a murderer.

After his drink, he inquired about a room. The barkeep gestured upstairs. "Second door on the right. If you're planning to stay, speak with the mayor. Julius Engel. He don't like surprises."

That night, he slept in a narrow bed above the saloon, the mattress lumpy but better than the ground. Outside, the cicadas buzzed a steady tune. The breeze carried the scent of honeysuckle and earth. No shouting. No gunfire. Just the soft hush of a town that didn't know his name.

He woke at dawn with his hand on his pistol, heart pounding. It was nothing—just a bird on the windowsill. But the instinct remained. He sat up, breathing slow, and stared out over the rooftops of Boerne.

Maybe he'd stay a day or two. Maybe longer.

He wasn't sure what drew him to this place—maybe it was the quiet. Maybe it was the way the girl outside the store looked at him like he was trouble she wasn't afraid of. Maybe it was just the way the town didn't feel broken.

He strapped on his guns and headed downstairs.

The townsfolk avoided his eyes that morning, but not out of fear. It was more like caution. Like they were giving him a chance. That was rare. He respected it.

He stopped by the blacksmith's to ask about a new saddle girth and ended up helping a boy shoe his first horse. He didn't say much, but the kid beamed all the same.

By noon, he'd spoken to Mayor Engel, who greeted him in a tidy office above the apothecary. Engel was older, clean-shaven, with spectacles perched on his nose and a Bible on his desk.

"You've got a reputation," the mayor said, offering him a seat.

"I try not to lean on it," Hickok replied.

"Well, let's keep it that way. We don't need shootouts or legends. We need peace."

"That's all I'm after."

The mayor studied him for a moment, then nodded. "Fine. You stay out of trouble, Mr. Hickok, and we won't have any."

With that, the conversation was over. Hickok left the office and wandered to the edge of town, where the cypress trees grew thick around a clear creek. He sat under the shade, hat tilted forward, and let the silence wash over him.

He didn't know it yet, but Boerne was about to change everything. The town, the girl, the storm coming in the hills—they would carve his future from the stone of this quiet place.

And for once, he wasn't running from it.

He was riding toward it.

Chapter Two: The General Store Girl

The morning sun broke clean over the rooftops of Boerne, casting long beams across cobbled streets and warming the limestone walls of the town's sturdy buildings. Wild Bill Hickok stepped out of the saloon's side door, stretching his legs and rolling the stiffness from his shoulders. He was used to the road—nights under the stars, mornings with stiff joints and the sound of coyotes in the distance—but waking up in a bed, even a lumpy one, was a small luxury.

The townsfolk were already about their business. A pair of boys wrestled in the dirt by the livery stable. A cart clattered by with sacks of flour and dried beans, and the baker's chimney was sending up ribbons of woodsmoke that smelled faintly of cinnamon. For a gunslinger, this was a strange kind of heaven.

He found himself walking back toward the general store—the one with the stone steps and the girl with the sharp eyes and sharper tongue. He wasn't sure why. Maybe it was curiosity. Maybe something else he wasn't ready to name.

She was there again, sweeping the steps just like before. But this time, when she saw him coming, she didn't stop. She just glanced up briefly, then went back to her broom.

"You sweep like it's a duel," Hickok said, leaning against the hitching post.

"And you talk like a man who wants trouble," she answered without looking up. Her hair was pinned neatly, but a few strands had escaped and framed her face in soft waves. The morning light caught the gold in her brown eyes.

"Name's Hickok," he said. "James Butler. But most folks call me Wild Bill."

She straightened, leaning on her broom. "I know who you are. Everyone does."

"Is that so?"

She nodded. "The butcher said you shot five men in one day. The barber said it was seven. My father says stories grow longer than shadows at sunset."

"And what do you say?"

She considered him for a moment. "I say you carry too much weight in your eyes to be proud of killing."

He let out a low breath. "You're not wrong."

She wiped her hands on her apron and extended one. "Klara Vogel."

Her grip was firm, confident. Hickok couldn't help but smile.

"So, Miss Vogel—this your store?"

"My father's. He came from Stuttgart ten years ago. Built it stone by stone. I help him run it, but one day it'll be mine."

He nodded, impressed. "Honest work. That's rare."

"We like things simple here," she said, brushing dust off the steps. "We grow. We build. We stay out of trouble."

"And I suppose I look like trouble."

"You look like someone who brings it with him."

A moment of silence passed between them. Then Klara pointed toward a crate by the door. "If you're so interested in the store, help me move that inside. It's flour, and it's heavy."

Hickok hesitated for a second—then shrugged and stepped forward, lifting the crate with ease. He followed her into the cool interior of the store, where the air smelled of coffee beans, leather, and dried herbs.

Inside, shelves were stacked with canned goods, bolts of cloth, tools, and books in both English and German. A large wooden counter ran along the back wall, behind which stood a heavyset man with a bristly mustache and wire-rimmed spectacles.

"Klara, who's this?" he asked in German, eyeing Hickok.

She replied in the same language, too fast for Hickok to follow. The older man frowned, then gave a slow nod and offered a hand.

"Wilhelm Vogel," he said. "Welcome to Boerne."

"Hickok," he replied, shaking the man's hand. "I'm just passin' through."

Wilhelm studied him with the kind of look that weighed more than words. Then he turned to his daughter. "Make sure he pays if he buys anything."

Klara laughed. "Of course, Papa."

After helping with the crate, Hickok bought a pouch of tobacco and a tin cup. Klara wrapped them in brown paper, and he handed her two silver coins.

"You planning to stay long?" she asked as he turned to go.

"Not sure yet. This place… it feels different."

"It is. But it stays different because people work to keep it that way."

He gave a slight nod. "Maybe I can help with that."

Outside, the town bustled quietly. Hickok walked down the street, the weight of the tobacco in his pocket a small reminder that maybe, just maybe, he could find something more than dust and regret in this town.

Over the next few days, he kept finding reasons to visit the store. A canteen that needed patching. A piece of jerky. A conversation. Klara was always there, always working. But she started to smile when she saw him, and once, she laughed at something he said. That laugh stayed with him.

The townsfolk began warming to him too. The blacksmith asked him to help repair a wagon axle. The pastor invited him to a community supper. The schoolteacher asked if he might speak to the children about the dangers of the frontier.

And always, Klara was there—watching him. Testing him.

One afternoon, as he helped her carry sacks of grain from the wagon, she asked, "Do you ever think of settling?"

He hesitated. "Never had much reason to."

"And now?"

"I don't know. Maybe I'm startin' to."

She looked at him then—not like a girl watching a gunslinger, but like a woman seeing the man behind the legend.

In that moment, Boerne stopped being just another dot on the map. It began to feel like a crossroads.

Not the end of the trail.

The beginning.

Chapter Three: Trouble on the Horizon

The sky above Boerne had shifted. What had once been tranquil skies and soft breezes now hinted at tension, like a violin string drawn just a note too tight. Wild Bill Hickok could feel it. Years of drifting through wild towns, dusty trails, and outlaw-ridden borders had given him a sixth sense for oncoming trouble. And something about the way the birds went quiet before noon, or how the men at the saloon leaned in too close over their whiskey, told him it was coming.

He sat outside the blacksmith's shop, whittling at a piece of cedar. Across the way, Klara was unloading dry goods from a new shipment, her brow furrowed in concentration. She glanced his way every now and then, her look more thoughtful than flirtatious.

Boerne had settled into a rhythm since his arrival. Hickok helped where he could—chopping wood for the church, fixing fences, and even watching the general store when Wilhelm took deliveries out to the ranches. Some of the older men in town were still wary, but the children adored him. He had started telling tall tales about coyotes with gold teeth and jackrabbits that robbed stagecoaches— stories that made the schoolhouse echo with laughter.

But now, the laughter had faded. A rider had come through three days earlier, covered in trail dust and sweat. He had barely taken time to water his horse before spreading the news that a gang calling themselves the Sandstone Boys had hit the bank in Kerrville—killed a teller, wounded the sheriff, and disappeared into the hills.

The townspeople were jittery. Boerne had never had much use for a formal lawman. They relied on tight community bonds and a little good fortune. But now, with rumors swirling and the distant sound of hooves too frequent for comfort, old rifles were being cleaned, and folks were whispering about bringing in the Texas Rangers.

Hickok knew better. He knew the kind of men who robbed banks and trains. Men who didn't fear badges because they'd already made peace with hell.

That afternoon, Klara found him in the shade behind the livery stable, oiling his Colt.

"You think they'll come here?" she asked.

He didn't look up. "They're heading west. Boerne's a soft stop. Small bank. No law. Plenty of horses."

"So what do we do?"

He holstered the revolver and met her eyes. "We get ready."

Later that evening, Hickok called a meeting at the church. The pews filled slowly—farmers, shopkeepers, the preacher, Wilhelm, even a few teenagers looking to play hero. The sun filtered through the stained-glass windows, throwing red and gold across worried faces.

Hickok stood at the pulpit. He hadn't stood in a church since he was a boy in Illinois, but the gravity of the moment held him tall.

"These men—if they come—aren't going to play fair. They're killers. Fast ones. They'll take what they want unless we stop them."

A murmur ran through the crowd.

"We're not soldiers," said an old man near the back. "We're farmers."

"You don't need to be soldiers," Hickok replied. "You need to be neighbors who stand together. I'll take the lead, but I can't do it alone."

The pastor stepped forward. "We've defended our homes from Comanche raids. We've rebuilt after floods. We'll do this too."

Plans were laid that night. Positions assigned. Rifles handed out. Wilhelm offered the general store as a makeshift headquarters, and Klara kept the register open longer than usual, handing out salt pork and coffee like ammunition.

The next day, Hickok rode out with two boys—one with good eyes, the other good ears—to scout the trails to the east. They found hoof prints in dry washes and cigarette butts under a sycamore. The gang was close. Too close.

Back in town, barricades were quietly prepared. Wagons filled with hay bales were rolled in front of the bank and post office. A few women learned how to reload shotguns, and children were moved to the church basement. Klara refused to stay behind.

"I'm not some damsel in a dime novel," she said. "If this town is to be defended, I'll do my part."

Hickok didn't argue. He just handed her a pistol and showed her how to keep her elbow steady when she fired.

That night, as the air cooled and the moon lit the rooftops like silver, Klara found him sitting outside the general store, cleaning his guns again.

"Do you ever get tired of fighting?" she asked.

"Every damn day," he replied without looking up.

"Then why keep doing it?"

He paused. "Because there's always someone who needs the fight done for them."

She sat beside him. "This isn't your town."

"Maybe not. But you're here. That's reason enough."

Their eyes met, and for a moment, time slowed. It wasn't love yet—not exactly. But it was its spark.

In the stillness of that night, before gunfire and thunder, Wild Bill Hickok began to feel something he hadn't in years.

Hope.

Chapter Four: When the Dust Rolled In

It began with thunder—not from the sky, but from the earth. The faint, rhythmic pounding of hooves, felt through the soles of one's boots before it ever reached the ears. Wild Bill Hickok stood on the rooftop of the saloon with a spyglass in one hand and his rifle propped beside him. He didn't speak. He didn't move. He just stared into the distance where a dust cloud billowed on the horizon.

"They're coming," he muttered.

Down below, townsfolk moved into position. Wilhelm was behind the counter in the general store, rifle in hand. The pastor and a few others crouched inside the church with shotguns and prayers. Klara stood at the window of the general store's second floor, pistol ready, eyes sharp. She had tied her hair back and rolled up her sleeves, looking more like a soldier than a shopkeeper's daughter.

The Sandstone Boys—seven riders in all—broke through the treeline just before noon. Dirty, hard-eyed men, their horses foaming with sweat, their faces wrapped in bandanas. Their leader, a broad-shouldered man with a black hat and a scar running from his left eye to his jaw, raised his hand, and the group slowed.

They trotted into town like they owned it.

Hickok tracked them from above. He recognized the leader from the scout's description: "Scarface Tom," a former Confederate scout turned outlaw, known for his fast draw and ruthless style.

Tom dismounted in front of the bank and motioned for two of his men to flank him. As they moved, Hickok fired his first shot.

Crack.

One of the riders collapsed backward off his horse, clutching his chest.

Pandemonium erupted. The gang scattered, returning fire in all directions. Townsfolk responded with a volley of rifle shots from windows and doorways. The ambush had begun.

Hickok moved like a machine. Reload. Fire. Move. He slid down the ladder at the back of the saloon and took cover behind a water trough. Bullets whined overhead, striking wood and stone.

Scarface Tom was shouting orders, trying to regroup. He ducked behind a wagon and fired twice at the church steeple, sending splinters raining down.

Inside the general store, Klara fired through the window, hitting another outlaw in the leg. He dropped to the ground with a scream, his gun skittering away across the dirt.

Wilhelm joined her, his heavy hunting rifle booming with each shot. "We hold them here!" he barked, sweating through his shirt. "For Boerne!"

The firefight stretched into an hour. Smoke filled the air, and the smell of gunpowder mixed with sweat and fear. Two townsfolk were injured—a boy named Eli with a grazed shoulder and an older man with a broken leg from falling down cellar steps—but no one had yet been killed.

Hickok spotted Scarface Tom sprinting for the post office and followed. He kicked down the back door just as Tom turned to fire.

The two men faced off in the dim light. Silence pressed in. The world narrowed to just the creak of the floorboards and the pounding of Hickok's heart.

Tom drew.

So did Hickok.

Two shots echoed almost simultaneously.

Tom staggered, hit square in the chest. Hickok's left arm went numb as a bullet grazed his shoulder. He winced, then walked forward slowly as Tom fell to his knees.

"You… damn legend," Tom hissed, coughing blood.

"Wrong town," Hickok replied, then watched as Tom slumped over, lifeless.

Outside, the remaining gang members were retreating. Without their leader, their courage had broken. A few tried to ride off but were stopped by rifle fire from the hills—where the town's younger boys, including the two scouts, had set up a surprise position.

By sundown, the battle was over.

Boerne was safe.

The townsfolk gathered outside the church, bruised and dirty but alive. Hickok stood at the center, blood seeping through his torn sleeve. Klara rushed to him, checking his wound.

"You idiot," she whispered, eyes wet with relief.

"Just a scratch," he said through gritted teeth.

Wilhelm walked over, silent for a long moment. Then he extended a hand. "You saved my daughter. And our town. I owe you more than I can say."

Hickok shook it, nodding.

Later that night, as stars filled the sky, a fire was lit in the town square. Folks brought out food, drink, and instruments. They sang songs in English and German, celebrated survival, and remembered the dead.

Klara found Hickok sitting on a bench, arm bandaged, sipping slowly from a tin cup.

"I can't decide if you're the bravest man I've met," she said, sitting beside him, "or the most foolish."

"Bit of both, maybe."

She looked up at the stars. "You don't have to leave, you know."

He didn't answer right away.

"You've seen the worst of us now," she continued. "But also the best."

"I've seen both in you," he said, turning to her. "And I want more of it."

She smiled, then leaned in, pressing her forehead to his. "Then stay."

He closed his eyes, breathing in the scent of her hair, the sound of laughter rising around them like a promise.

And in that moment, Wild Bill Hickok—gunslinger, drifter, loner—felt something new:

Home.

Chapter Five: The Quiet After the Storm

The morning after the battle, the town of Boerne woke under a veil of smoke and silence. Ashes drifted like snow through the crisp dawn air, and broken glass shimmered on the main street like spilled stars. The church bell rang not in celebration, but in solemn remembrance. Though the town had survived, its scars were fresh.

Hickok rose before the sun. His shoulder throbbed with pain, but he ignored it, pulling his shirt gingerly over the bandage. He stepped out onto the porch of the boarding house where he'd been staying and took in the stillness. Birds chirped cautiously from the trees, uncertain if it was safe to sing again.

He made his way down the road, past townsfolk sweeping debris from doorways and righting overturned barrels. Children who had been hidden away during the fight now peeked from behind their mothers' skirts, wide-eyed and curious.

Outside the general store, Wilhelm was already at work repairing a shattered window. His jaw was set tight, but there was a calm determination in his movements. Klara was inside, straightening shelves and restocking what little had been knocked loose. When she saw Hickok, she stepped outside and met him with a soft smile.

"Morning," she said.

"Morning," he replied. "How's the town?"

"Shaken, but proud. You gave them that. We all did."

They stood for a moment, the air between them thick with unspoken words. Then she nodded toward the back of the store.

"Coffee's on. Come sit."

Inside, the familiar aroma of fresh grounds wrapped around Hickok like a blanket. He settled into a chair while Klara poured two mugs. They sipped in silence.

"Do you think they'll come back?" she asked quietly.

Hickok's eyes narrowed. "If there's one thing I've learned, it's that cowards like them don't come back unless they think no one's watching. We'll stay ready. But I don't think we'll see the Sandstone Boys again."

She nodded. "Good."

The door opened, and Wilhelm entered, wiping sweat from his brow. He paused when he saw Hickok and gave him a short nod of respect.

"I've seen what you can do with a gun, Mr. Hickok," he said. "But today, we could use your hands for something else."

"Name it."

"Help me rebuild the front. Show the town you're more than just a fast draw."

Hickok stood and rolled up his sleeve with a half-smile. "Lead the way."

The next few hours were spent hammering nails, cutting boards, and lifting beams. Word of Hickok's help spread quickly. By midday, he wasn't the only volunteer—dozens of townsfolk had gathered to repair homes and businesses alike. The town, once fearful, had found strength in its unity.

Children ran about delivering water to the workers. An older woman hummed a German lullaby while sewing a torn flag. At one point, the town's pastor brought out his guitar and played soft tunes that drifted through the streets like a balm.

It wasn't just rebuilding—it was healing.

As the sun dipped low in the sky, Klara brought out a basket of bread and sausages. She and Hickok sat together again, this time on the store's wooden steps, sharing their meal.

"I never thought I'd see you swinging a hammer," she said, nudging his shoulder.

"I never thought I'd like it," he admitted.

She looked at him for a long moment. "What did you think you'd find in Texas?"

He hesitated. "Peace. Or at least a place where my name didn't matter."

"And did you?"

"I found something better."

Their eyes met. The sounds of hammering and music filled the silence between them, but it felt like the world had gone still.

Later that night, as dusk painted the sky in amber and violet, Wilhelm stood before the gathered townsfolk outside the church.

"We owe our lives to each other," he said. "This town stood together. And we stand stronger now."

He raised a hand toward Hickok. "This man came to us a stranger. He risked everything for people he didn't know. And now, he's one of us."

There was a chorus of cheers, followed by the sound of glasses clinking and laughter. Hickok, standing at the edge of the crowd, looked down, touched by the simple sincerity of it.

Klara found him again.

"You've got friends here now," she said.

"Feels strange," he said. "Good. But strange."

"Get used to it."

They watched the firelight dance on the faces of their neighbors. Somewhere in the background, someone began to sing an old folk tune. The melody was unfamiliar to Hickok, but the warmth of it felt like home.

That night, he didn't return to the boarding house. He followed Klara through the quiet streets to the back porch of her home. They sat in the silence of crickets and creaking boards.

"I think I'd like to stay," he said at last.

"I think I'd like that too," she whispered.

And as they sat there, two souls weathered by life but softened by love, Boerne's newest chapter quietly began.

The days following the battle slipped into a fragile calm, but Wild Bill Hickok knew better than most that peace in a frontier town was often only the quiet before the storm. Boerne was healing, yes — roofs patched, windows replaced, laughter returning — but somewhere beyond the hills, in the shadowed stretches of brush and canyon, a darker force was gathering strength.

Hickok had become a fixture in town, no longer a mysterious drifter but a protector and friend. His mornings began with coffee and a glance over the ridge, scanning the hills where trouble often lurked. Evenings found him talking quietly with Klara on the porch of her family's home, the soft glow of lanterns framing her face like a beacon.

One morning, Wilhelm came to him with news. His brow was furrowed, hands clenched over a rolled-up newspaper.

"There's talk of another gang," Wilhelm said grimly. "Lurking near Comfort, they've been robbing stagecoaches and small farms. They call themselves the Black Vultures."

Hickok frowned. The Black Vultures were rumored to be even more ruthless than the Sandstone Boys—merciless men with little regard for human life. If they set their sights on Boerne, it wouldn't be just a robbery. It would be a massacre.

"We need to prepare," Hickok said.

Wilhelm nodded. "We'll need every able-bodied man. But this town—" He gestured toward the peaceful streets, "—they've seen too much. I don't know if they'll stand again."

Hickok's eyes darkened. "They will. They have to."

That afternoon, he and Klara walked through the town square, speaking quietly with shopkeepers and farmers. The mood was cautious. Some expressed fear, others anger, but many showed determination. The battle had forged a new spirit in Boerne—a refusal to be cowed.

By sunset, a town meeting had been called in the church. Men and women gathered in the pews, their faces marked by worry but lit with resolve. Hickok stood before them, his voice steady and commanding.

"We've faced down Scarface Tom and the Sandstone Boys. Now a new threat rides in the shadows—the Black Vultures. They don't care for life or honor. But neither do we."

He paused, scanning the crowd. "We will defend our homes. We'll train, we'll organize, and we'll stand together. No one rides through Boerne unchallenged."

Wilhelm stood beside him, adding, "Klara and I will help train the women and children in what to do if trouble comes. Everyone has a part to play."

Over the next week, the town transformed. Hickok led shooting drills at the edge of the woods, teaching sharpshooting and cover tactics. Wilhelm organized patrols. Klara taught the women to load pistols and tend wounds. Children practiced messages and hiding places.

One afternoon, as Hickok worked on his aim beneath the scorching Texas sun, a figure approached from the ridge—barely more than a shadow against the dry grass. It was the scout who'd warned of Scarface Tom's gang.

"I found something," the scout said, breathless. "Tracks. Black Vultures. They're closer than we thought—just past the old mill, moving toward the railway."

Hickok's jaw tightened. "They're coming."

That night, under the blanket of stars, the town was restless. Fires flickered, rifles rested by doorways, and eyes watched every shadow. Klara sat beside Hickok, her hand in his.

"What if it's worse this time?" she whispered.

Hickok squeezed her hand. "Then we'll be ready. Together."

The next days were a blur of preparation and waiting. Scouts patrolled the hills, reports came and went, and tension hung in the air like a storm cloud ready to burst.

Then, one evening as the sun dipped low, the distant sound of hooves thundered over the ridge.

Black dust rose against the fading light.

The Black Vultures had arrived.

Chapter Seven: The Siege of Boerne

The first sign of trouble came just as dawn broke over the rolling Texas hills—a sharp, echoing gunshot that split the morning air like a knife. It was the alarm, and it sent a ripple through the heart of Boerne. Wild Bill Hickok, already awake and alert, grabbed his rifle and moved toward the town square, where the men were gathering, eyes sharp, hands ready.

The Black Vultures were upon them.

From the ridge, a cloud of dust signaled the advance of the gang— rough riders clad in black, faces masked beneath scarves, eyes cold and merciless. Their horses thundered down the slope, a living wall of menace. Hickok stood tall, his rifle aimed, waiting for the first sign.

The townsfolk were ready, but only just. The training from the past weeks had taught them much, yet none had faced such a well-armed, vicious band before. Wilhelm was at Hickok's side, leading a group of men toward the bank, a prime target for the outlaws. Klara, pistol holstered, coordinated the women who had taken up roles guarding the homes and tending to the wounded.

As the Vultures rode into town, the battle erupted in a fury of smoke and steel. Gunfire cracked from both sides, horses reared and shouted rang out. Hickok's voice was a steady anchor amidst the chaos.

"Hold your ground! Protect the people!"

Bullets tore through the wooden buildings, splinters flying as townsfolk ducked behind barrels and wagon wheels. The Black Vultures were ruthless, using every tactic to break the defenders' spirit—setting fires, charging homes, and aiming for the weakest.

Hickok moved with practiced precision, firing from the porch of the general store, then ducking into cover as return fire answered. His left arm still bore the scar from the last fight, but the pain was swallowed by adrenaline.

At one point, a group of Vultures surged toward the bank. Wilhelm and a few men formed a barricade, trading fire and holding the line as best they could. The bank's heavy doors shook under repeated kicks and rifle butts, threatening to give way.

Inside the church, the pastor rallied a band of townsfolk, praying and tending to the injured, but ready to fight if the walls were breached.

Klara was everywhere—loading rifles, treating wounds, calming frightened children. Her resolve was fierce, and her aim deadly. She took down two of the attackers who tried to force their way into her family's home.

Hours stretched on like a nightmare. The sun climbed high and began to fall again, but the fighting showed no sign of abating. Hickok realized that the Vultures had come not just for money, but for control—this was a warning to Boerne and every town nearby.

As exhaustion began to claim the defenders, Hickok called for a strategic retreat to the town's center, where they could make a final stand. The church steps became a rallying point, its stone walls providing cover and hope.

"We can't let them win!" Hickok shouted, voice hoarse. "For Boerne!"

The townsfolk's fire was rekindled. They pushed back with renewed energy, firing in unison, forcing the Vultures to fall back bit by bit.

In the thick of the fight, Hickok spotted a figure moving swiftly—one of the gang's leaders attempting to flank the defenders and set fire to the stables. Without hesitation, Hickok pursued, firing shots that rang out sharp and true.

The outlaw turned, pistols drawn. The duel was brief, deadly—a flash of gunfire, a cry, and the man fell, clutching his chest.

But the victory was bittersweet. The stables burned, horses whinnied in panic, and the town's supply of fresh mounts was reduced.

As dusk approached, the fighting slowed. The Black Vultures, battered and leaderless after Hickok's relentless pursuit, began to withdraw. The townsfolk, though weary and wounded, had held their ground.

Wilhelm approached Hickok, his face lined with dirt and sweat but glowing with gratitude.

"You saved us again," he said quietly.

Klara stepped forward, her eyes shining with fierce pride. "Boerne will not fall."

That night, the town gathered once more, tending wounds and mourning losses. The battle had taken a toll—several injured and two men lost—but the spirit of Boerne burned brighter than ever.

Hickok sat beside Klara, their hands entwined.

"We did it," she said softly.

"For now," he replied, eyes scanning the dark horizon. "But I don't think this is the last they'll come for us."

And so, under the canopy of stars and the watchful eyes of a town reborn, Wild Bill Hickok and Boerne prepared for the challenges yet to come.

Chapter Eight: Bonds Forged in Fire

The sun rose on Boerne with a promise of new beginnings, but the scars of the siege remained deeply etched in the town's heart and buildings. The air still carried the acrid scent of smoke and burnt wood. Broken fences and shattered windows marked the paths where the Black Vultures had stormed through like a whirlwind of destruction. Yet, amid the ruins, there was an undeniable pulse of resilience—a determination to rebuild, stronger and closer than ever.

Wild Bill Hickok moved through the town like a man carrying the weight of both victory and loss. His broad shoulders, still scarred from the fights, bore the burden of leadership none had asked for but all had come to rely upon. Today was not a day for rest. The hard work of repair, recovery, and preparation awaited.

At the general store, Wilhelm was already organizing supplies for rebuilding efforts. His hands, though roughened by years of hard labor, worked with precision and care. Klara was nearby, tending to a group of children who had returned to their routines but still clung nervously to their mothers. Her presence was a balm to the shaken souls of the town.

Hickok joined them, the early morning light catching the faint glint of resolve in his eyes.

"We need to keep training," he said. "The Black Vultures will be back if we show weakness. But more than that, we need to heal. This town has fought hard and lost some good people. That pain can either break us or bind us."

Wilhelm nodded solemnly. "I agree. But we must also be vigilant. Word is spreading about Boerne's stand. We're becoming a symbol—a beacon. That will draw more trouble as much as it draws hope."

Klara smiled faintly, though her eyes reflected the hardships of recent weeks. "Then we'll face it together. Like family."

And family was exactly what the people of Boerne were becoming. That afternoon, a meeting was called in the town hall, not just of men but of women and children, elders and newcomers. Stories were shared—of bravery, of loss, of the stubborn hope that kept them going.

Hickok spoke openly, not as the legendary gunslinger he once was, but as a man invested in the lives around him.

"We all have scars," he said quietly. "Visible and invisible. But scars are proof we survived. And that means we have a future."

The room filled with nods, some tearful, some fierce.

Among the crowd, Klara caught his eye. She approached later, her voice low and steady. "You've changed this town—and me. I can't imagine Boerne without you."

Hickok looked at her, the weight of unspoken feelings hanging between them. "Neither can I."

Days turned into weeks as rebuilding continued. Hickok and Wilhelm supervised repairs, working side by side with carpenters, blacksmiths, and farmers. Klara organized community efforts—teaching first aid, sharing stories that soothed, and rallying spirits with her quiet strength.

The bond between Hickok and Klara deepened with every shared task and every stolen moment beneath the vast Texas sky. They were no longer just two souls who met by chance—they were partners in a town's survival and its future.

One evening, as the sun dipped below the horizon, casting the sky in streaks of gold and crimson, Hickok and Klara stood together overlooking the town square. Lanterns flickered to life, and the sounds of children's laughter echoed through the streets once more.

"Do you ever think about the life we might have had if we'd never met?" Klara asked softly.

Hickok smiled, a rare softness in his gaze. "I don't think about the past much anymore. The future is what matters. And this—" he gestured toward the town, "—this is where I want to be."

She leaned her head on his shoulder. "Me too."

But even as peace settled over Boerne, shadows lingered beyond the hills. The Black Vultures were not finished, and new dangers awaited. Yet in that moment, forged in fire and hardship, the people of Boerne—and Wild Bill Hickok—stood ready to face whatever came next.

The warm days of spring brought with them a fragile sense of calm to Boerne. Flowers bloomed along the dusty streets, and the town's battered buildings wore fresh coats of paint. Children ran through the square with wide smiles, their laughter a balm to the weary souls who had fought so hard to protect their home.

Wild Bill Hickok had settled into a rhythm—mornings spent working with Wilhelm on town projects, afternoons training the militia, and evenings with Klara, whose quiet strength had become the cornerstone of his new life. They were no longer just lovers but partners, bound by shared trials and the promise of something more enduring than the gunfights and chaos that had marked his past.

Yet, beneath the surface of this hard-won peace, a tension simmered. Boerne was no longer a quiet town; it was a symbol of defiance in a lawless land. And symbols attract attention— sometimes dangerous attention.

One afternoon, as Hickok helped repair the roof of the church, a rider approached from the west. His horse was exhausted, and his face was pale with urgency.

"Mr. Hickok," the rider gasped, handing over a folded letter. "From Comfort."

Hickok unfolded the paper quickly, his eyes scanning the words. The letter spoke of increasing outlaw activity—more raids, more violence. The Black Vultures had not only survived their defeat in Boerne but had grown bolder. Worse, a new gang was emerging from the east, threatening towns along the trade routes.

Wilhelm joined Hickok, reading over his shoulder with a frown. "It's spreading. The peace we fought for is fragile."

That night, a town meeting was called. The church was packed with men, women, and even some of the town's youth, all eager to hear what must be done.

"We have two choices," Hickok began, his voice steady but serious. "We can barricade ourselves behind these walls and hope the outlaws pass us by. Or we can take the fight to them, protect not just Boerne but the entire region."

The room fell silent. The stakes had never been higher.

Klara stood and spoke with quiet conviction. "We've built something here. A home, a community. But if we wait for the next attack, we risk losing everything."

Wilhelm added, "We need allies. Letters have been sent to neighboring towns. It's time to unite."

Plans were made to strengthen defenses, train harder, and send scouts to gather intelligence. Hickok and Wilhelm volunteered to lead a delegation to meet with other town leaders—a dangerous journey, but necessary.

In the weeks that followed, the town pulled together like never before. The wounds of the siege slowly healed, but the price of peace became clear. Supplies were scarce, the threat of betrayal loomed, and every day brought news of new dangers.

One evening, as Hickok and Klara sat beneath a sprawling oak, she reached for his hand.

"Do you ever regret staying?" she asked softly.

Hickok looked at her, his eyes reflecting the weight of his past and the hope for their future. "Every day, I'm grateful. But peace isn't free. It's paid for in vigilance, sacrifice, and sometimes heartbreak."

Their moments of quiet joy were precious but fleeting. A week later, word came that a small neighboring settlement had been attacked, its people taken or killed. The harsh reality of the frontier pressed in.

The delegation departed at dawn, riders cutting through the hills with determination. Hickok led the way, Wilhelm by his side. They carried the hopes of Boerne—and the promise that no town would stand alone against the darkness creeping across the land.

As they disappeared into the horizon, Klara stood in the town square, watching with a mixture of pride and fear. She whispered a prayer for their safe return and for the fragile peace that depended on their courage.

Chapter Ten: A Legacy Written in Blood and Hope

The sun was low in the sky, casting long shadows over Boerne as Wild Bill Hickok rode slowly into town. His horse's steady gait was a quiet contrast to the storm of memories swirling in his mind. The journey with Wilhelm and the delegation had been arduous—weeks spent riding through unforgiving terrain, meeting with wary town leaders, and facing threats from both outlaws and the harsh land itself. But it had been a necessary mission. The fragile alliance they forged along the dusty roads was the first step toward a united front against the growing lawlessness.

As Hickok approached the main street, he saw Klara waiting by the porch of the general store. Her eyes lit up with a mixture of relief and unspoken worry. When he dismounted, she rushed forward, her arms wrapping around him in a fierce embrace.

"You're back," she whispered, her voice trembling with emotion.

"I'm home," he replied, the simple words carrying the weight of everything he had come to mean by them.

The years that followed were ones of hard work and quiet determination. Boerne grew from a battered frontier settlement into a thriving community, its streets bustling with merchants, craftsmen, and families who called this place home. The alliance of towns, born out of Hickok's delegation, held strong, creating a network of mutual defense and shared resources.

Hickok himself became more than a legend; he became a pillar of the community. He trained the town's militia, taught the children how to shoot straight and act with honor, and worked alongside Wilhelm to ensure the town's prosperity. But the peace they built was never guaranteed—outlaws still lurked in the shadows, and the frontier always held dangers.

Klara's role grew alongside his. She became a leader in her own right, organizing aid for the injured, supporting the families of those lost, and managing the general store that had become a lifeline for the town. Together, they raised their children amidst stories of courage and sacrifice, teaching them the values that had saved Boerne.

Yet, the shadow of the past was never far away. On quiet nights, Hickok would find himself staring at the stars, remembering the battles, the friends lost, and the choices that had shaped his path. The gun was still by his side, a reminder that peace was hard-won and could be lost in an instant.

One evening, as a soft breeze rustled the leaves, Hickok sat on the porch with Klara and their eldest son, a boy who already showed the steady hand and sharp eyes of his father.

"Tell me about the old days," the boy asked, eyes wide with curiosity.

Hickok smiled, his gaze distant but warm. "There were times when the world was darker, when a man's strength was measured by the courage in his heart and the steadiness of his hand. But it's not just about fighting—it's about standing up for what's right, even when it's hard."

Klara leaned against him, her hand resting on his. "And it's about family. That's what makes a place a home."

The legacy of Wild Bill Hickok in Boerne was more than tales of gunfights and battles. It was a story of transformation—a gunslinger who found something worth fighting for beyond the draw of the gun. It was about a town that refused to bow to fear, bound together by hope and resilience.

As the stars blanketed the Texas sky, Hickok knew that their story was far from over. But for now, in the quiet strength of a family and a town reborn, there was peace.

And that peace was a legacy worth leaving.

Welcome & Thank You!

Thank you so much for purchasing this book from **R&E Publishing** — we're truly grateful for your support! We hope you're enjoying the content and finding it both entertaining and enriching.

Your feedback means everything to us. If you've enjoyed this book, we kindly ask that you take a moment to **leave a review and rating on Amazon**. Your reviews help other readers discover our books and allow us to continue creating more of the content you love.

At R&E Publishing, we're passionate about crafting engaging, thoughtful, and fun books across a variety of genres — from puzzles and educational activity books and more. Be sure to check out our other titles available on Amazon and grow your collection today!

If you have any **questions, suggestions, or concerns**, we'd love to hear from you. Please don't hesitate to contact us directly at:

RandE.PublishingHouse@gmail.com

Once again, thank you for being a valued reader. Your support makes all the difference, and we look forward to bringing more enjoyable reads your way!

Warm regards,
The R&E Publishing Team